OLD MAN, GOODBYE

A Farewell to the Old Man of the Mountain

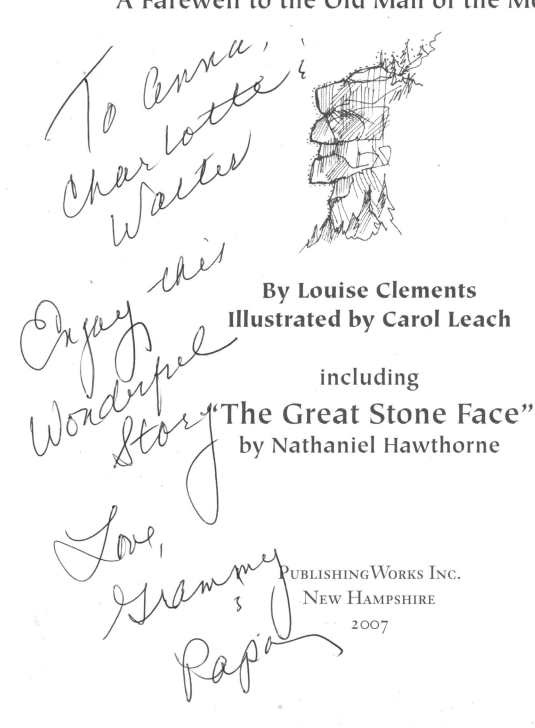

Handwritten inscription: To Anna, Charlotte & Walter, Enjoy this Wonderful Story. Love, Grammy & Rapa

By Louise Clements
Illustrated by Carol Leach

including
"**The Great Stone Face**"
by Nathaniel Hawthorne

PublishingWorks Inc.
New Hampshire
2007

Fifth Printing, 2007

Published by:

PublishingWorks, Inc.
60 Winter Street
Exeter, NH 03833
603/778-9883
800/333-9883

Sales:
Revolution Booksellers, LLC
60 Winter Street
Exeter, NH 03833
1-800-REV-6603
www.revolutionbooksellers.com
Type set in Calisto MT. Display type is Tiepolo.

Printed in Canada.

Library of Congress Cataloging-in-Publication Data
Clements, Louise.
   Old Man, goodbye : a farewell to the Old Man of the Mountain / by Louise Clements ; illustrated by
Carol Leach. The Great Stone Face / by Nathaniel Hawthorne.
   p. cm.
   Summary: When nine-year-old Ernest and his father travel to New Hampshire to say goodbye to the stone
formation known as the Old Man of the Mountain, Ernest experiences the peace of the woods, listens to his
father tell Nathaniel Hawthorne's story of "The Great Stone Face," and has a mysterious encounter.
   ISBN: 0-9744803-0-4
   ISBN13: 978-0-9744803-0-5
   [1. Old Man of the Mountain (N.H.)--Fiction. 2. Fathers and sons--Fiction. 3. New Hampshire--Fiction.]
I. Leach, Carol, ill. II. Hawthorne, Nathaniel, 1804-1864. III. Title.
   PZ7.C591501 2003
   [Fic]--dc22   2003190058

Dedicated to the memory of
The Old Man

Prologue

The following story about Ernest and his dad was written just a few days after the Old Man fell on May 3, 2003. Those days were filled with shock and sadness.

Carol Leach began to draw her illustrations soon after she read the story. The book was published by: Publishing Works in Exeter, New Hampshire and the first books were delivered on November first in 2003. They have the distinction of being the first in print after the Old Man's fall and this is the only book that describes the feelings of people after we lost the Old Man to memories and history.

The story is fiction but it is a definitive book for New Hampshire's memories of the Old Man.

A Little History

Our **Old Man of the Mountain** was up on Cannon Mountain when early colonists arrived. Yes, he was there looking down at snow-covered mountains in winter. He was there when the ice in rivers and lakes melted. He was there to welcome birds when they migrated north as they do each spring. He was there on warm summer nights when the moon was round and owls hunted and he was there when the trees turned to their spectacular autumn colors.

The granite that is here in New Hampshire today was covered by an ice sheet that covered New Hampshire thousands of years ago. During those years, nature created our Old Man of the Mountain.

Nathaniel Hall, a member of a survey group building a road through Franconia Notch, looked up to see The Old Man of the Mountain's profile high up on Cannon Mountain. This happened in 1805. Ever since that day stories, poems and ballads have been written about our Old Man, and thousands of people have come to gaze at his profile on Cannon Mountain.

In 1945 The Old Man of the Mountain became the Official Emblem of the State of New Hampshire, and over the years many people have spent their time and efforts caring for the mighty profile on Cannon Mountain.

In 1954 cracks on the top of the Old Man's head were getting wider and additional maintenance work began. Adolphus Bowles was in charge of the work. Niels F. Nielsen, Jr., took part in all the repair efforts and in 1965 took over this monumental task from Adolphus Bowles.

Niels Nielsen conducted repairs on the south face and was one of the first to descend the Old Man's forehead. He was named the Old Man's Official Caretaker in 1987 and his son, David Nielsen, was named Official Caretaker in 1991.

To these brave, caring and courageous men
we say a very special
Thank You!

New York City, has many tall buildings and is crowded with a lot of traffic. Cars, trucks and busses are on all the streets.

Ernest and his family lived on the fifth floor in an apartment building near a hospital.

Ernest especially liked it when his father, a doctor, came home early from the hospital. On those special days when it was sunny they walked to Central Park where they pretended they were mountain climbers. They hiked and climbed on large rocks.

One day as they sat on a big flat rock Dad said, "Would you like to hike on some real mountain trails this summer?"

"Really? Can we? That would be super great!"

Dad said, "I was thinking it would be fun to drive up to New Hampshire and spend three days hiking and climbing mountain trails." He reached into his pocket and pulled out what looked like a shiny gold coin and gave it to Ernest.

"This is a coin that can be used to pay a toll on a New Hampshire highway. Take a look, Ernest, what do you see?"

"It looks like a man's head on both sides."

"That's right. It's the Old Man of the Mountain. Nature formed him out of rocks on top of Cannon Mountain. Tourists come from all over to see him. He's been there for many years. He's famous! We'll say hello to him when we go to New Hampshire. My Dad took me to see him when I was about your age Ernest, so now I want to take you."

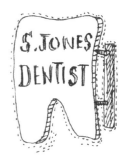

Ernest was happy and excited! This would be a great adventure!

On nights when Ernest's dad was home at bedtime, he always read a story to Ernest. Now instead of reading they talked about their trip to New Hampshire. Dad sent away for camping information and when it arrived they had fun deciding where they wanted to stay. They finally decided to stay in a log cabin. It had bunk beds. Dad wanted to sleep on the top bunk. The cabin had a table and chairs, a tiny kitchen, an indoor fireplace and outside it had a fireplace for grilling hamburgers and hotdogs. Ernest was so excited he could almost taste the hotdogs with lots of ketchup, of course!

One evening Ernest's Dad told him a story about Daniel Webster, a well known United States Senator. Senator Webster once said that dentists hung signs with a tooth on them to indicate what they did, shoemakers hung signs with a shoe to advertise that they worked with shoes, and up there in New Hampshire they use the profile of the Old Man of the Mountain to show how strong and rugged the people are in that state! Ernest liked to hear stories about New Hampshire.

April 15 arrived – Ernest's ninth birthday! After school Ernest and three of his friends went to Central Park. The day was sunny and warm. Mom and Dad planned a scavenger hunt in the park and the treasure was four red bandanas and a compass for Ernest and each of his friends. Later they had pizza, ice cream and cake.

At bedtime Dad brought Ernest a special present. It was a very old book with stories written by Nathaniel Hawthorne. It used to belong to Ernest's grandfather. "My father gave this to me when I was nine years old," Dad told him. "And now I am giving it to you. We won't begin to read tonight but when we go to New Hampshire we'll take it with us and then I will read you the story my dad read to me when I was your age. We'll read it in the cabin and we will find the Old Man of the Mountain and say hello to him."

"Thanks, Dad," Ernest said, yawning. "I can't wait to see the Old Man!"

May 3, 2003 was a Saturday. Grandma came to take Ernest to Central Park in the afternoon because Mom had work to do at home and Dad was at the hospital.

Later that evening Ernest was building with his Legos in his room when he heard his dad come home from the hospital. He heard his mom and dad talking in the kitchen where Mom was making a pie for Sunday dinner. It was about 8:30 P.M. Ernest heard Dad say, "I'm going to talk to him now. This is going to be difficult."

Ernest looked up when he saw his Dad standing in his doorway. "Hi Dad," he said, feeling uneasy when he saw his father's sad face.

"May I come in, Ernest? I have some news for you that will be difficult for us both." Dad looked serious as he crouched down next to Ernest. "I have to tell you something that I never dreamed I would be telling you. The Old Man fell down the mountain today. He's no longer 1,200 feet high on Cannon Mountain. He's in pieces at the bottom on the shores of Profile Lake." Dad paused and seemed to be fighting back tears. "He was a great symbol of the rugged people who live in New Hampshire. He was their true spirit of the Granite State. I am sad that you and I won't be able to see him when we go to New Hampshire."

"Why did he fall? What happened to him?"

"This winter was extremely cold with lots of snow. Snow melts on warm days, water gets into the cracks, then it gets cold again, the water freezes and when ice forms it expands and the cracks get wider. This happens year after year and this year came along and weakened the Old Man and so he fell. Nature created the Old Man and nature took him away. He was cherished, and we're sad that he is gone, but he will be remembered."

Ernest thought about what his dad said. "I think we should go to New Hampshire just as we planned and when we're there, we'll say goodbye to the Old Man."

"I'm glad you still want to go," Dad said. "I do too."

Ernest put away his Legos, he said good night to his mom and dad. He put on his pajamas and was ready to climb into bed but first he saw the New Hampshire token that was on his table next to his bed. He picked it up and hopped in bed with the token in his hand.

THE DAY finally arrived. Ernest and his dad were in the car and ready to roll at 5:00 A.M. They drove north through Connecticut and Massachusetts, stopping along the highway for breakfast. Back in the car, Ernest said, "Dad, it sure seems like a long time to get there!" Dad laughed. "It's always longer when you're excited about getting to where you're going, isn't it?" Finally, they saw a sign welcoming them to the Granite State. Soon after, they saw the State House in Concord with its gold dome, and later the mountains in the distance. Now there were tall trees on both sides of the highway, the sun was shining, the sky was blue, it was a lovely day! They looked for the exit they were supposed to take and followed their directions until they saw the sign for Smith Cabins. They drove along a dirt road for a mile and came to a campground where they saw a dozen small log cabins standing among tall pines. They pulled up to a larger cabin with a sign over the door that read Office. A man came out to welcome them. He smiled and told them he was Ed Smith. He pointed to one of the cabins and told them they would have cabin number 3. He followed them as they drove over and parked the car next to the cabin. A squirrel

6

scampered off the porch and sat on top of the outdoor fireplace.

"You might want to buy some peanuts when you go to the local store," Mr. Smith told them. "The people who were here last week fed this little fellow, so he's pretty tame."

Mr. Smith showed Ernest and his dad where to find extra blankets if they needed them and how to work the gas stove. There was cut and stacked wood next to the indoor fireplace. The cottage was perfect in every way! When they had finished unpacking, they decided to find the store.

The store was owned by a man named Snow. There was a sign over the doorway that said, Snow's Country Store. Inside, the shelves were packed with all sorts of items. They bought hamburger, hotdogs, marshmallows, apples, pears, bananas, milk and coffee for the blue coffee pot. And peanuts for the squirrel. Dad went to the counter to pay. "You have a good name for this part of the world, Mr. Snow. I hear you had a lot of it this winter."

"Yup, we sure did. I guess it was too much for our Old Man. We sure do miss him."

"I am sure you do. My son and I came up here to see him but now we will have to say goodbye to him instead."

IT TOOK a while to put all the things away when they returned to the cabin. When they finished they went out to explore the area. They walked along a path in the woods listening to bird calls.

"Listen, Ernest, an Ovenbird is calling. He says, 'teach, teach teach.' He's pretty loud but you don't see him often. He usually walks on the ground."

They heard a Blue Jay scolding and then they saw him. Just off the path they saw a lovely plant with a beautiful pink bloom. Dad told Ernest it was a Lady Slipper. The pine needle scent was strong as they walked along the path.

When they were hungry, they went back to the cabin for dinner. Mom had made them a stew for their first night's dinner, and cookies for dessert. After they finished and washed the dishes, they sat on the cabin steps with the book by Nathaniel Hawthorne. In it was the story called, "The Great Stone Face."

"It's a story about a boy named Ernest," Dad said.

"Really! Like me!"

"That's right. Ernest lived in a cabin with his mother just below Cannon Mountain. They could see the Old Man of the Mountain every day. In those days long ago they didn't have television to watch, or a radio to listen to. He didn't have games to play on his computer. Life was quiet. Ernest walked in the woods, helped his mother and looked up at the Old Man of the Mountain.

8

He and the Old Man of the Mountain became good friends. Can you now guess why your name is Ernest?" Dad asked.

"You named me after the story?"

"Yes. Mom and I both liked the name and I remembered it because my Dad took me to New Hampshire and read me Nathaniel Hawthorne's story."

Ernest was delighted to hear he was named for a boy in a story. It was sort of special. Dad said, "I am not going to read tonight. I think we're pretty tired. Let's go inside and light a small fire because the marshmallows are calling my name."

Ernest thought he could hear them calling to him, too. The fire leaped up and lighted the inside of the cabin. Outside the evening light slipped through the trees. Ernest and his dad put on their pajamas while the fire settled down and the coals were ready for toasting. The marshmallows were especially good. After teeth were brushed they climbed into their bunks. Ernest watched the glowing coals and soon both Ernest and his dad were asleep.

The next day after breakfast they sat on the steps of their cabin while Dad enjoyed his second cup of coffee. They began reading "The Great Stone Face." Ed Smith walked over to say good morning and listened to a bit of the story, too.

9

Dad asked Mr. Smith where they should go for a hike and he told them to turn left when they came to the main road and drive four miles to the trail's parking area. "There's a nice trail that goes through some marshy land near a small pond.

After the pond you will see a Great Blue Heron rookery on the right. The birds are still there. After the rookery the trail will climb and give you a good hike."

They made peanut butter sandwiches and put them in their backpacks along with apples and Mom's cookies. They filled their canteens with water, put on their hiking boots and set off to find the trail.

Soon they were walking on a spongy path through the marshy land that Mr. Smith told them about. Ernest was in front leading the way, and he saw something scurry right in front of him. He stopped and the something flew to a branch just ahead of them. It was a bird about the size of a chicken, with a black belly and white stripes along his sides. A white line ran down his neck and his tail had a yellowish tip. There was a small red patch above his eye. The bird sat there and just looked at Ernest and his dad. He didn't seem the least bit afraid. They looked at each other for a long time. Finally, Dad whispered, "Ernest, you have just met your first Spruce Grouse."

They walked on and saw the Great Blue Heron Rookery and counted eleven nests in the tall trees. They enjoyed their picnic in a clearing along the trail. It was a wonderful hiking day and when they returned to their cabin Ernest fed the squirrel who was waiting for them on the cabin porch.

Hotdogs were on the menu for dinner. Soon they had their outdoor fireplace going and the hotdogs tasted really good with lots of ketchup, of course!

After dinner clean up they sat down to read.

"The Great Stone Face" tells of a prophecy. A man, some man, was supposed to arrive in the valley. He was supposed to look like the Old Man of the Mountain. The boy in the story, Ernest, heard about this prophecy and he too waited for this special man to arrive. Three men did arrive one after the other, but each of these men turned out not to be that special person.

The boy grew to be a man. He continued to live in his cabin year after year and he continued to work and he continued to grow older. People liked him, they knew he was a good person. He wasn't famous or rich, but people who knew him trusted him and they liked to listen to him talk. People knew he was honest and kind. He was a good man. Each evening after he finished working in his fields he sat in front of his cabin and looked up at the Old Man of the Mountain. Sometimes in the evenings he would sit on a rock and his friends would gather around and

listen to his stories. On one evening there was a famous poet in the group who declared that Ernest looked like the Old Man of the Mountain.

People looked at Ernest and they agreed. He did resemble the Old Man of the Mountain. The prophecy had come true! Ernest was a modest man. He knew Old Man of the Mountain was a mighty being and he never would pretend that he was equal to his friend way up there on top of Cannon Mountain. He thanked the poet for his thoughts then he took him by the arm and they walked back to his cabin.

ERNEST and his Dad hadn't realized that Mr. Smith had joined them to listen to Nathaniel Hawthorne's story. He sat quietly nearby on a stump. When Dad closed the book Mr. Smith said, "That's a mighty good story. It just goes to prove that you don't have to be famous or rich to live a good life."

"That's very true," Dad said.

Mr. Smith said good night and walked over to where he lived behind his office. Ernest and his Dad were sleepy, they got ready for bed and climbed into their bunks. They listened to the Wood Thrush sing his fluting notes as they closed their eyes.

The next morning they packed some ham and cheese sandwiches and the last of Mom's cookies and set off for Profile Lake. They spent the day with the memory of the Old Man of the Mountain

high above. They skipped stones in the lake and enjoyed being part of nature. Finally, as they drove back to their cabin Dad said, "I am glad we were able to come to New Hampshire. Being up here in the woods reminds me that people don't need a lot of things to be happy. We should all try to make the world a little bit better, a little bit nicer."

They stopped at Mr. Snow's store to pick up a few things for their dinner. It was a fine feast.

They roasted potatoes and ate juicy hamburgers with watermelon slices. Ice cream sandwiches were followed by more toasted marshmallows. The air smelled of pine. It was quiet and peaceful in the New Hampshire woods.

The next morning Ernest took some photographs of their cabin. He put peanuts on the porch to coax the squirrel, who posed for him.

Ernest and his dad decided to try another hiking trail. It was pretty flat for a while, following a stream, but after they crossed the shallow water, hopping from rock to rock, the trail was steep with boulders on each side. They climbed higher and higher and higher. When they came to a clearing and a lookout, they stopped to look down at the stream far below.

They also had a good view of Mt. Washington in the distance, the highest mountain in New Hampshire. Dad told Ernest that when a car drives all the way to the 6,288 foot peak, the driver gets a bumper sticker that says, "This Car Climbed Mt. Washington." They climbed higher after

they rested a bit and when they were hungry they climbed on to a large boulder with a flat surface and ate their sandwiches. It was peaceful and beautiful. High in the sky they saw a Great Blue Heron flapping its wings. "I bet I know where he's going," said Ernest.

They reluctantly climbed down the mountain to head back to their cabin for their last night. Tomorrow they would be leaving these woods to go home to New York City.

It was about three in the afternoon when they reached their cabin and Dad had to use Mr. Smith's office phone to call the hospital and home.

"Dad, while you're making your calls I want to photograph the Lady Slipper we saw. It's not far away and I think Mom will like a picture of it because it's so different."

"Great idea. I'll wait for you on the porch."

As Ernest started along the path he and Dad took the day they arrived, he heard an Oven Bird calling, 'teach, teach, teach'. He came to the Lady Slipper and took its picture for his mom and then he took another for his scrapbook. It was shady and cool in the woods. The pine needles were thick on the path. Ernest sat down on them and leaned against the trunk of a tree. He was a bit sleepy after the hike and closed his eyes, but only for a second or two. He heard a small branch crack as if someone stepped on it and opened his eyes. There before him stood an old man.

14

He wore a leather vest over his long-sleeved shirt. His trousers were torn and his boots were scratched. His face was wrinkled, his nose wasn't absolutely straight, his forehead stuck out and so did his chin. Even his neck was full of wrinkles. He looked stern, but he smiled kindly. It wasn't a big wide open, teeth-showing smile. It was sort of a thin-lipped, friendly smile. He leaned on a stick he used as a cane.

"Hello, Ernest. I am glad you enjoy nature's treasures well enough to want to remember this beautiful day."

"How did you know my name?" Ernest managed to ask.

"Oh, I've been around these parts for a long, long time," the old man answered. "It's nice you came here, Ernest. The mountains are majestic. They give you strength to understand the power of nature."

Ernest looked at the old man's wrinkled face. His face was amazing! He blinked and the old man was gone!

Ernest hurried back to the cabin where Dad was sitting on the porch feeding the squirrel.

"Dad, do you want to see the Lady Slipper again?" Ernest really wanted to go back to see if the old man was still around.

"Well, ok, I'll take another look and then I'll start a fire. We'll finish up the hotdogs this evening."

Ernest and Dad walked into the woods to look at the Lady Slipper. Dad said it was a lovely treasure. The old man had called it a treasure, too.

"Look, Ernest, it's a good thing we came. You dropped your New Hampshire token. Here put it back in your pocket." Ernest reached into his right pocket and pulled out the token Dad had given him.

"Well, I'll be darned," Dad said, amazed. "Another token out here in the woods. Someone must have dropped it."

Ernest thought he knew who had, but it was all very strange and he decided not to say anything.

They went back to the cabin, made a fire in the indoor fireplace and roasted hotdogs with toasted marshmallows for dessert.

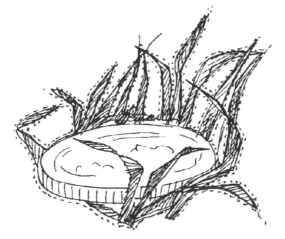

The next morning they packed after breakfast. Dad had his second cup of coffee and Ernest fed the squirrel the rest of the peanuts. They went to the office to say thank you and goodbye to Mr. Smith and as they drove down the dirt road Ernest said, "Dad, do we have time to drive by Profile Lake? We can toss our tokens into the lake as a special farewell to the Old Man of the Mountain."

"That's a wonderful idea!"

So Ernest and his dad stood on the shore of Profile Lake. They looked up to the top of Cannon Mountain and tossed their tokens into the lake saying their special goodbye to the Old Man of the Mountain, whose spirit will live on and on...

A Note from the Author

The story you just read was written in 2003. "The Great Stone Face," by Nathaniel Hawthorne, was written long ago. There were no computers in those days and a mouse was a little gray creature who ate cheese. Nathaniel Hawthorne used some words we don't use very often. For instance, Hawthorne used the word "visage" when he wrote about the Old Man's profile. Nathaniel Hawthorne's vocabulary is perhaps a bit antique, but "The Great Stone Face" is a wonderful story. When Ernest's dad read the story to him, Ernest liked it and so did Ed Smith.

When was the last time your mother, dad, grandparent or any older person read to you? Now you can read by yourself, but try reading "The Great Stone Face" along with an older person. Remember, you don't have to read the whole story in one sitting. Take your time and discuss the story as you read. The person with you also may want to read. That would be nice. You might want to have a dictionary nearby in case you want to find the definition of a word. When the three men arrive one at a time, discuss their characteristics. What was Mr. Gathergold like? What was Old Blood–and–Thunder like? And, what was Old Stony Phiz really like? Reading is an important thing to do so talk about the story and enjoy yourselves. If you do this you will make the Old Man very happy!

The Great Stone Face

Nathaniel Hawthorne
1804-1864

Nathaniel Hawthorne visited the Old Man of the Mountain in 1832, and later immortalized him in "The Great Stone Face." This story is one of a collection called *Twice Told Tales.*

Nathaniel Hawthorne was a lifelong friend of Franklin Pierce, the fourteenth president of the United States. Hawthorne's friends included Poe, Emerson, Thoreau, Longfellow, and Melville. These men were all authors and they all lived in or near Boston, Massachusetts about the same time. Herman Melville inscribed his book, *Moby-Dick* to Hawthorne, "In token of my admiration."

The state emblem adopted in 1945
featuring the Old Man.

ONE AFTERNOON, when the sun was going down, a mother and her little boy sat at the door of their cottage, talking about the Great Stone Face. They had but to lift their eyes, and there it was plainly to be seen, though miles away, with the sunshine brightening all its features.

And what was the Great Stone Face?

Embosomed amongst a family of lofty mountains, there was a valley so spacious that it contained many thousand inhabitants. Some of these good people dwelt in log-huts, with the black forest all around them, on the steep and difficult hillsides. Others had their homes in comfortable farm-houses, and cultivated the rich soil on the gentle slopes or level surfaces of the valley. Others, again, were congregated into populous villages, where some wild, highland rivulet, tumbling down from its birthplace in the upper mountain region, had been caught and tamed by human cunning, and compelled to turn the machinery of cotton-factories. The inhabitants of this valley, in short, were numerous, and of many modes of life. But all of them, grown people and children, had a kind of familiarity with the Great Stone Face, although some possessed the gift of distinguishing this grand natural phenomenon more perfectly than many of their neighbors.

The Great Stone Face, then, was a work of Nature in her mood of majestic playfulness, formed on the perpendicular side of a mountain by some immense rocks, which had been thrown together in such a position as, when viewed at a proper distance, precisely to resemble the features of the human countenance. It seemed as if an enormous giant, or a Titan, had sculptured his own likeness on the precipice. There was the broad arch of the forehead, a hundred feet in height; the nose, with its long bridge; and the vast lips, which, if they could have spoken, would have rolled their thunder accents from one end of the valley to the other. True, it is, that if the spectator approached too near, he lost the outline of the gigantic visage, and could discern only a heap of ponderous and gigantic rocks, piled in chaotic ruin one upon another. Retracing his steps, however, the wondrous features would again be seen; and the farther he withdrew from them, the more like a human face, with all its original divinity intact, did they appear; until, as it grew dim in the distance, with the clouds and glorified vapor of the mountains clustering about it, the Great Stone Face seemed positively to be alive.

It was a happy lot for children to grow up to manhood or womanhood with the Great Stone Face before their eyes, for all the features were noble and the expression was at once grand and sweet, as if it were the glow of a vast, warm heart, that embraced all mankind in its affections, and had room for more. It was an education only to look at it. According to the belief of many people, the valley owed much of its fertility to this benign aspect that was continually beaming over it, illuminating the clouds, and infusing tenderness into the sunshine.

As we began with saying, a mother and her little boy sat at their cottage door, gazing at the Great Stone Face, and talking about it. The child's name was Ernest.

"Mother," said he, while the Titanic visage smiled on him, "I wish that it could speak, for it looks so very kindly that its voice must needs be pleasant. If I were to see a man with such a face, I should love him dearly."

"If an old prophecy should come to pass," answered his mother, "we may see a man, some time or other, with exactly such a face as that."

"What prophecy do you mean, dear mother?" eagerly inquired Ernest. "Pray tell me all about it!"

So his mother told him a story that her own mother had told to her, when she herself was younger than little Ernest; a story, not of things that were past, but of what was yet to come; a story, nevertheless, so very old, that even the Indians, who formerly inhabited this valley, had heard it from their forefathers, to whom, as they affirmed, it had been murmured by the mountain streams, and whispered by the wind among the tree-tops. The purport was, that, at some future day, a child should be born hereabouts, who was destined to become the greatest and noblest personage of his time, and whose countenance in manhood should bear an exact resemblance to the Great Stone Face. Not a few old-fashioned people, and young ones likewise, in the ardor of their hopes, still cherished an enduring faith in this old prophecy. But others, who had seen more of the world, had watched and waited till they were weary, and had beheld no man with such a face, nor any man that proved to be much greater or nobler than his neighbors, concluded it to be nothing but an idle tale. At all events, the great man of the prophecy had not yet appeared.

"O mother, dear mother!" cried Ernest, clapping his hands above his head, "I do hope that I shall live to see him!"

His mother was an affectionate and thoughtful woman, and felt that it was wisest not to discourage the generous hopes of her little boy. So she only said to him, "Perhaps you may."

And Ernest never forgot the story that his mother told him. It was always in his mind, whenever he looked upon the Great Stone Face. He spent his childhood in the log-cottage where he was born, and was dutiful to his mother and helpful to her in many things, assisting her much with his little hands and more with his loving heart. In this manner, from a happy yet often pensive child, he grew up to be a mild, quiet, unobtrusive boy, and sun-browned with labor in the fields, but with more intelligence brightening his aspects than is seen in many lads who have been taught at famous schools. Yet Ernest had had no teacher, save only that the Great Stone Face became one to him. When the toil of the day was over, he would gaze at it for hours, until he began to imagine that those vast features recognized him, and gave him a smile of kindness and encouragement, responsive to his own look of veneration. We must not take upon us to affirm that this was a mistake, although the Face may have looked no more kindly at Ernest than at all the world besides. But the secret was, that the boy's tender and confiding simplicity discerned what other people could not see; and thus the love, which was meant for all, became his peculiar portion.

About this time, there went a rumor throughout the valley, that the great man, foretold from ages long ago, who was to bear a resemblance to the Great Stone Face, had appeared at last. It seems that, many years before, a young man had migrated from the valley and settled at a distant seaport, where, after getting together a little money, he had set up as a shopkeeper. His name—but I could never learn whether it was his real one, or a nickname that had grown out of his habits and success in life—was Gathergold. Being shrewd and active, and endowed by Providence with that inscrutable faculty which develops itself in what the world calls luck, he became an exceedingly rich merchant, and owner of a whole fleet of bulky-bottomed ships. All the countries of the globe appeared to join hands for the mere purpose of adding heap after heap to the mountainous accumulation of this one man's wealth. The cold regions of the North, almost within the gloom and shadow of the Arctic Circle, sent him their tribute in the shape of furs; hot Africa sifted for him the golden sands of her rivers, and gathered up the ivory tusks of her great elephants out of the forests; the East came bringing him the rich shawls, and spices, and teas, and the effulgence of diamonds, and the gleaming purity of large pearls. The ocean, not to be behindhand with the earth, yielded up her mighty whales that Mr. Gathergold might sell their oil, and make a profit on it. Be the original commodity what it might, it was gold within his grasp. It might be said of him as of Midas in the fable, that whatever he touched with his finger immediately glistened, and grew yellow, and was changed at once into sterling metal, or, which suited him still better, into piles of coin. And, when Mr. Gathergold had become so very rich that it would have taken him a hundred years only to count his wealth, he bethought himself of his native valley, and resolved to go back thither, and end his days where he was born. With this purpose in view, he sent a skilful architect to build him such a palace as should be fit for a man of his vast wealth to live in.

As I have said above, it had already been rumored in the valley that Mr. Gathergold had turned out to be the prophetic personage so long and vainly looked for, and that his visage was the perfect and undeniable similitude of the Great Stone Face. People were the more ready to believe that this must needs be the fact, when they beheld the splendid edifice that rose, as if by enchantment, on the site of his father's old weather-beaten farmhouse. The exterior was of marble, so dazzling white that it seemed as though the whole structure might melt away in the sunshine, like those humbler ones which Mr. Gathergold, in his young play-days, before his fingers were gifted with the touch of transmutation, had been accustomed to build of snow.

It had a richly ornamented portico, supported by tall pillars, beneath which was a lofty door, studded with silver knobs, and made of a kind of variegated wood that had been brought from beyond the sea. The windows, from the floor to the ceiling of each stately apartment, were composed, respectively, of but one enormous pane of glass, so transparently pure that it was said to be a finer medium than even the vacant atmosphere. Hardly anybody had been permitted to see the interior of this palace; but it was reported, and with good semblance of truth, to be far more gorgeous than the outside, insomuch that whatever was iron or brass in other houses was silver or gold in this; and Mr. Gathergold's bed-chamber, especially, made such a glittering appearance that no ordinary man would have been able to close his eyes there. But, on the other hand, Mr. Gathergold was now so inured to wealth, that perhaps he could not have closed his eyes unless where the gleam of it was certain to find its way beneath his eyelids.

In due time the mansion was finished; next came the upholsterers, with magnificent furniture; then, a whole troop of black and white servants, the harbingers of Mr. Gathergold, who, in his own

majestic person, was expected to arrive at sunset. Our friend Ernest, meanwhile, had been deeply stirred by the idea that the great man, the noble man, the man of prophecy, after so many ages of delay, was at length to be made manifest to his native valley. He knew, boy as he was, that there were a thousand ways in which Mr. Gathergold, with his vast wealth, might transform himself into an angel of beneficence, and assume a control over human affairs as wide and benignant as the smile of the Great Stone Face. Full of faith and hope, Ernest doubted not that what the people said was true, and that now he was to behold the living likeness of those wondrous features on the mountain-side. While the boy was still gazing up the valley, and fancying, as he always did, that the Great Stone Face returned his gaze and looked kindly at him, the rumbling of wheels was heard, approaching swiftly along the winding road.

"Here he comes!" cried a group of people who were assembled to witness the arrival. "Here comes the great Mr. Gathergold!"

A carriage, drawn by four horses, dashed round the turn of the road. Within it, thrust partly out of the window, appeared the physiognomy of a little old man, with a skin as yellow as if his own Midas-hand had transmuted it. He had a low forehead, small, sharp eyes, puckered about with innumerable wrinkles, and very thin lips, which he made still thinner by pressing them forcibly together.

"The very image of the Great Stone Face!" shouted the people. "Sure enough, the old prophecy is true; and here we have the great man come, at last!"

And, what greatly perplexed Ernest, they seemed actually to believe that here was the likeness which they spoke of. By the roadside there chanced to be an old beggar-woman and two little beggar-children, stragglers from some far-off region, who, as the carriage rolled onward, held out their hands and lifted up their doleful voices, most piteously beseeching charity. A yellow claw—the very same that had clawed together so much wealth—poked itself out of the coach-window, and dropped some copper coins upon the ground; so that, though the great man's name seems to have been Gathergold, he might just as suitably have been nicknamed Scattercopper. Still, nevertheless, with an earnest shout, and evidently with as much good faith as ever, the people bellowed,—

"He is the very image of the Great Stone Face!"

But Ernest turned sadly from the wrinkled shrewdness of that sordid visage, and gazed up the valley, where, amid a gathering mist, gilded by the last sunbeams, he could still distinguish those glorious features which had impressed themselves into his soul. Their aspect cheered him. What did the benign lips seem to say?

"He will come! Fear not, Ernest; the man will come!"

The years went on, and Ernest ceased to be a boy. He had grown to be a young man now. He attracted little notice from the other inhabitants of the valley; for they saw nothing remarkable in his way of life, save that, when the labor of the day was over, he still loved to go apart and gaze and meditate upon the Great Stone Face. According to their idea of the matter, it was a folly indeed, but pardonable, inasmuch as Ernest was industrious, kind, and neighborly, and neglected no duty for the sake of indulging this idle habit. They knew not that the Great Stone Face had become a teacher to him, and that the sentiment which was expressed in it would enlarge the young man's heart, and fill it with wider and deeper sympathies than other hearts. They knew not that thence would come a better wisdom than could be learned from books, and a better life than could be moulded on the defaced example of other human lives. Neither did Ernest know that the thoughts and affections which came to him so naturally, in the fields and at the fireside, and wherever he communed with himself, were of higher tone than those which all men shared with him. A simple soul,—simple as when his mother first taught him the old prophecy,—he beheld the marvellous features beaming adown the valley, and still wondered that their human counterpart was so long in making his appearance.

By this time poor Mr. Gathergold was dead and buried; and the oddest part of the matter was, that his wealth, which was the body and spirit of his existence, had disappeared before his death, leaving nothing of him but a living skeleton, covered over with a wrinkled, yellow skin. Since the melting away of his gold, it had been very generally conceded that there was no such striking resemblance, after all, betwixt the ignoble features of the ruined merchant and that majestic face upon the mountain-side. So the people ceased to honor him during his lifetime, and quietly consigned him to forgetfulness after his decease. Once in a while, it is true his memory was brought up in connection with the magnificent palace which he had built, and which had long ago been turned into a hotel for the accommodation of strangers, multitudes of whom came, every summer, to visit that famous natural curiosity, the Great Stone Face. Thus, Mr. Gathergold being discredited and thrown into the shade, the man of prophecy was yet to come.

It so happened that a native-born son of the valley, many years before, had enlisted as a soldier, and, after a great deal of hard fighting, had now become an illustrious commander. Whatever he may be called in history, he was known in camps and on the battlefield under the nickname of Old Blood-and-Thunder. This war-worn veteran, being now infirm with age and wounds, and weary of the turmoil of a military life, and of the roll of the drum and the clangor of the trumpet, that had so long been ringing in his ears, had lately signified a purpose of returning to his native valley, hoping to find repose where he remembered to have left it. The inhabitants, his old neighbors and their grown-up children, were resolved to welcome the renowned warrior with a salute of cannon and a public dinner; and all the more enthusiastically, it being affirmed that now, at last, the likeness of the Great Stone Face had actually appeared. An aide-de-camp of old Blood-and-Thunder, travelling through the valley, was said to have been struck with the resemblance. Moreover, the schoolmates and early acquaintances of the general were ready to testify, on oath, that, to the best of their recollection, the aforesaid general had been exceedingly like the majestic image, even when a boy, only that the idea had never occurred to them at that period. Great, therefore, was the excitement throughout the valley; and many people, who had never once thought of glancing at the Great Stone Face for years before, now spent their time in gazing at it, for the sake of knowing exactly how General Blood-and-Thunder looked.

On the day of the great festival, Ernest, with all the other people of the valley, left their work, and proceeded to the spot where the sylvan banquet was prepared. As he approached, the loud voice of the Reverend Doctor Battleblast was heard, beseeching a blessing on the good things set before them, and on the distinguished friend of peace in whose honor they were assembled. The tables were arranged in a cleared space of the woods, shut in by the surrounding trees, except where a vista opened eastward, and afforded a distant view of the Great Stone Face. Over the general's chair, which was a relic from the home of Washington, there was an arch of verdant boughs, with the laurel profusely intermixed, and surmounted by his country's banner, beneath which he had won his victories. Our friend Ernest raised himself on his tip-toes, in hopes to get a glimpse of the celebrated guest; but there was a mighty crowd about the tables anxious to hear the toasts and speeches, and to catch any word that might fall from the general in reply; and a volunteer company, doing duty as a guard, pricked ruthlessly with their bayonets at any particularly quiet person among the throng. So Ernest, being of an unobtrusive character, was thrust quite into the background, where he could see no more of Old Blood-and-Thunder's physiognomy than if it had been still blazing on the battle-field. To console himself, he turned towards the Great Stone Face, which, like a faithful and long-remembered friend, looked back and smiled upon him through the vista of the forest. Meantime, however, he could overhear the remarks of various individuals, who were comparing the features of the hero with the face on the distant mountain-side.

"'Tis the same face, to a hair!" cried one man, cutting a caper for joy.

"Wonderfully like, that's a fact!" responded another.

"Like! Why, I call it Old Blood-and-Thunder himself, in a monstrous looking-glass!" cried a third. "And why not? He's the greatest man of this or any other age, beyond a doubt."

And then all three of the speakers gave a great shout, which communicated electricity to the crowd, and called forth a roar from a thousand voices, that went reverberating for miles among the mountains, until you might have supposed that the Great Stone Face had poured its thunder-breath into the cry. All these comments, and this vast enthusiasm, served the more to interest our friend; nor did he think of questioning that now, at length, the mountain-visage had found its human counterpart. It is

true, Ernest had imagined that this long-looked-for personage would appear in the character of a man of peace, uttering wisdom, and doing good, and making people happy. But, taking an habitual breadth of view, with all his simplicity, he contended that Providence should choose its own method of blessing mankind, and could conceive that this great end might be effected even by a warrior and a bloody sword, should inscrutable wisdom see fit to order matters so.

"The general! The general!" was now the cry. "Hush! Silence! Old Blood-and-Thunder's going to make a speech."

Even so; for the cloth being removed, the general's health had been drunk amid shouts of applause, and he now stood upon his feet to thank the company. Ernest saw him. There he was, over the shoulders of the crowd, from the two glittering epaulets and embroidered collar upward, beneath the arch of green boughs with intertwined laurel, and the banner drooping as if to shade his brow! And there, too, visible in the same glance, through the vista of the forest, appeared the Great Stone Face! And was there, indeed, such a resemblance as the crowd had testified? Alas, Ernest could not recognize it! He beheld a war-worn and weather-beaten countenance, full of energy, and expressive of an iron will; but the gentle wisdom, the deep, broad, tender sympathies were altogether wanting in Old Blood-and-Thunder's visage; and even if the Great Stone Face had assumed his look of stern command, the milder traits would still have tempered it.

"This is not the man of prophecy," sighed Ernest to himself, as he made his way out of the throng. "And must the world wait longer yet?"

The mists had congregated about the distant mountain-side, and there were seen the grand and awful features of the Great Stone Face, awful but benignant, as if a mighty angel were sitting among the hills, and enrobing himself in a cloud-vesture of gold and purple. As he looked, Ernest could hardly believe but that a smile beamed over the whole visage, with a radiance still brightening, although without motion of the lips. It was probably the effect of the western sunshine, melting through the thinly diffused vapors that had swept between him and the object that he gazed at. But—as it always did—the aspect of his marvellous friend made Ernest as hopeful as if he had never hoped in vain.

"Fear not, Ernest," said his heart, even as if the Great Face were whispering to him,—"fear not, Ernest; he will come."

More years sped swiftly and tranquilly away. Ernest still dwelt in his native valley, and was now a man of middle age. By imperceptible degrees, he had become known among the people. Now, as heretofore, he labored for his bread, and was the same simple-hearted man that he had always been. But he had thought and felt so much, he had given so many of the best hours of his life to unworldly hopes for some great good to mankind, that it seemed as though he had been talking with the angels, and had imbibed a portion of their wisdom unawares. It was visible in the calm and well-considered beneficence of his daily life, the quiet stream of which had made a wide green margin all along its course. Not a day passed by, that the world was not the better because this man, humble as he was, had lived. He never stepped aside from his own path, yet would always reach a blessing to his neighbor. Almost involuntarily, too, he had become a preacher. The pure and high simplicity of his thought, which, as one of its manifestations, took shape in the good deeds that dropped silently from his hand, flowed also forth in speech. He uttered truths that wrought upon and moulded the lives of those who heard him. His auditors, it may be, never suspected that Ernest, their own neighbor and familiar friend, was more than an ordinary man; least of all did Ernest himself suspect it; but, inevitably as the murmur of a rivulet, came thoughts out of his mouth that no other human lips had spoken.

When the people's minds had had a little time to cool, they were ready enough to acknowledge their mistake in imagining a similarity between General Blood-and-Thunder's truculent physiognomy and the benign visage on the mountain-side. But now, again, there were reports and many paragraphs in the newspapers, affirming that the likeness of the Great Stone Face had appeared upon the broad shoulders of a certain eminent statesman. He, like Mr. Gathergold and Old Blood-and-Thunder, was a native of the valley, but had left it in his early days and taken up the trades of law and politics. Instead of the rich man's wealth and the warrior's sword, he had but a tongue, and it was mightier than both together. So wonderfully eloquent was he, that whatever he might choose to say, his auditors had no choice but to believe him; wrong looked like right, and right like wrong; for when it pleased him he could make a kind of illuminated fog with his mere breath, and obscure the natural daylight with it. His tongue, indeed, was a magic instrument: sometimes it rumbled like the thunder; sometimes it warbled like the sweetest music. It was the blast of war,—the song of peace; and it seemed to have a heart in it, when there was no such matter. In good truth he was a wondrous man; and when his tongue had acquired him all other imaginable success,—when it had been heard in halls of state, and in the courts of princes and potentates,—after it had made him known all over the world, even as a voice crying from shore to shore,—it finally persuaded his countrymen to select him for the presidency. Before this time,—indeed, as soon as he began to grow celebrated,—his admirers had found out the resemblance between him and the Great Stone Face; and so much were they struck by it, that throughout the country this distinguished gentleman was known by the name of Old Stony

Phiz. The phrase was considered as giving a highly favorable aspect to his political prospects; for, as is likewise the case with Popedom, nobody ever becomes president without taking a name other than his own.

While his friends were doing their best to make him president, Old Stony Phiz, as he was called, set out on a visit to the valley where he was born. Of course, he had no other object than to shake hands with his fellow-citizens, and neither thought nor cared about any effect which his progress through the country might have upon the election. Magnificent preparations were made to receive the illustrious statesman; a cavalcade of horsemen set forth to meet him at the boundary line of the State, and all the people left their business and gathered along the wayside to see him pass. Among these was Ernest. Though more than once disappointed, as we have seen, he had such a hopeful and confiding nature, that he was always ready to believe in whatever seemed beautiful and good. He kept his heart continually open, and thus was sure to catch the blessing from on high, when it should come. So now again, as buoyantly as ever, he went forth to behold the likeness of the Great Stone Face.

The cavalcade came prancing along the road, with a great clattering of hoofs and a mighty cloud of dust, which rose up so dense and high that the visage of the mountain-side was completely hidden from Ernest's eyes. All the great men of the neighborhood were there on horseback: militia officers in uniform; the member of Congress; the sheriff of the county; the editors of newspapers; and many a farmer too had mounted his patient steed, with his Sunday coat upon his back. It really was a very brilliant spectacle, especially as there were numerous banners flaunting over the cavalcade, on some of which were gorgeous portraits of the illustrious statesman and the Great Stone Face, smiling familiarly at one another, like two brothers. If the pictures were to be trusted, the mutual resemblance, it must be confessed, was marvellous. We must not forget to mention that there was a band of music, which made the echoes of the mountains ring and reverberate with the loud triumph of its strains; so that airy and soul-thrilling melodies broke out among all the heights and hollows, as if every nook of his native valley had found a voice, to welcome the distinguished guest.

But the grandest effect was when the far-off mountain precipice flung back the music; for then the Great Stone Face itself seemed to be swelling the triumphant chorus, in acknowledgment that, at length, the man of prophecy was come.

All this while the people were throwing up their hats and shouting, with enthusiasm so contagious that the heart of Ernest kindled up, and he likewise threw up his hat, and shouted, as loudly as the loudest, "Huzza for the great man! Huzza for Old Stony Phiz!" But as yet he had not seen him.

"Here he is, now!" cried those who stood near Ernest. "There! There! Look at Old Stony Phiz and then at the Old Man of the Mountain, and see if they are not as like as two twin-brothers!"

In the midst of all this gallant array came an open barouche, drawn by four white horses; and in the barouche, with his massive head uncovered, sat the illustrious statesman, Old Stony Phiz himself.

"Confess it," said one of Ernest's neighbors to him, "the Great Stone Face has met its match at last."

Now, it must be owned that, at his first glimpse of the countenance which was bowing and smiling from the barouche, Ernest did fancy that there was a resemblance between it and the old familiar face upon the mountain-side. The brow, with its massive depth and loftiness, and all the other features, indeed, were boldly and strongly hewn, as if in emulation of a more than heroic, of a Titanic model. But the sublimity and stateliness, the grand expression of a divine sympathy, that illuminated the mountain visage, and etherealized its ponderous granite substance into spirit, might here be sought in vain. Something had been originally left out, or had departed. And therefore the marvellously gifted statesman had always a weary gloom in the deep caverns of his eyes, as of a child that has outgrown its playthings, or a man of mighty faculties and little aims, whose life, with all its high performances, was vague and empty, because no high purpose had endowed it with reality.

Still, Ernest's neighbor was thrusting his elbow into his side, and pressing him for an answer.

"Confess! Confess! Is not he the very picture of your Old Man of the Mountain?"

"No!" said Ernest, bluntly, "I see little or no likeness."

"Then so much the worse for the Great Stone Face!" answered

35

his neighbor; and again he set up a shout for Old Stony Phiz.

But Ernest turned away, melancholy, and almost despondent; for this was the saddest of his disappointments, to behold a man who might have fulfilled the prophecy, and had not willed to do so. Meantime, the cavalcade, the banners, the music, and the barouches swept past him, with the vociferous crowd in the rear, leaving the dust to settle down, and the Great Stone Face to be revealed again, with the grandeur that it had worn for untold centuries.

"Lo, here I am, Ernest!" the benign lips seemed to say. "I have waited longer than thou, and am not yet weary. Fear not; the man will come."

The years hurried onward, treading in their haste on one another's heels. And now they began to bring white hairs and scatter them over the head of Ernest; they made reverend wrinkles across his forehead, and furrows in his cheeks. He was an aged man. But not in vain had he grown old: more than the white hairs on his head were the sage thoughts in his mind; his wrinkles and furrows were inscriptions that Time had graved, and in which he had written legends of wisdom that had been tested by the tenor of a life. And Ernest had ceased to be obscure. Unsought for, undesired, had come the fame which so many seek, and made him known in the great world, beyond the limits of the valley in which he had dwelt so quietly. College professors, and even the active men of cities, came from far to see and converse with Ernest; for the report had gone abroad that this simple husbandman had ideas unlike those of other men, not gained from books, but of a higher tone,—a tranquil and familiar majesty, as if he had been talking with the angels as his daily friends. Whether it were sage, statesman, or philanthropist, Ernest received these visitors with the gentle sincerity that had characterized him from boyhood, and spoke freely with them of whatever came uppermost, or lay deepest in his heart or their own. While they talked together, his face would kindle, unawares, and shine upon them, as with a mild evening light. Pensive with the fulness of such discourse, his guests took leave and went their way; and, passing up the valley, paused to look at the Great Stone Face, imagining that they had seen its likeness in a human countenance, but could not remember where.

While Ernest had been growing

up and growing old, a bountiful Providence had granted a new poet to this earth. He, likewise, was a native of the valley, but had spent the greater part of his life at a distance from that romantic region, pouring out his sweet music amid the bustle and din of cities. Often, however, did the mountains which had been familiar to him in his childhood lift their snowy peaks into the clear atmosphere of his poetry. Neither was the Great Stone Face forgotten, for the poet had celebrated it in an ode, which was grand enough to have been uttered by its own majestic lips. This man of genius, we may say, had come down from heaven with wonderful endowments. If he sang of a mountain, the eyes of all mankind beheld a mightier grandeur reposing on its breast, or soaring to its summit, than had before been seen there. If his theme were a lovely lake, a celestial smile had now been thrown over it, to gleam forever on its surface. If it were the vast old sea, even the deep immensity of its dread bosom seemed to swell the higher, as if moved by the emotions of the song. Thus the world assumed another and a better aspect from the hour that the poet blessed it with his happy eyes. The Creator had bestowed him, as the last, best touch to his own handiwork. Creation was not finished till the poet came to interpret, and so complete it.

The effect was no less high and beautiful, when his human brethren were the subject of his verse. The man or woman, sordid with the common dust of life, who crossed his daily path, and the little child who played in it, were glorified if he beheld them in his mood of poetic faith. He showed the golden links of the great chain that intertwined them with an angelic kindred; he brought out the hidden traits of a celestial birth that made them worthy of such kin. Some, indeed, there were, who thought to show the soundness of their judgment by affirming that all the beauty and dignity of the natural world existed only in the poet's fancy. Let such men speak for themselves, who undoubtedly appear to have been spawned forth by Nature with a contemptuous bitterness; she having plastered them up out of her refuse stuff, after all the swine were made. As respects all things else, the poet's ideal was the truest truth.

The songs of this poet found their way to Ernest. He read them, after his customary toil, seated on the bench before his cottage door, where, for such a length of time, he had filled his repose with thought, by gazing at the Great Stone Face. And now, as he read stanzas that caused the soul to thrill within him, he lifted his eyes to the vast countenance beaming on him so benignantly.

"O majestic friend," he murmured, addressing the Great Stone Face, "is not this man worthy to resemble thee?"

The Face seemed to smile, but answered not a word.

Now it happened that the poet, though he dwelt so far away, had not only heard of Ernest, but had meditated much upon his character, until he deemed nothing so desirable as to meet this man, whose untaught wisdom walked hand in hand with the noble simplicity of his life. One summer morning, therefore, he took passage by the railroad, and, in the decline of the afternoon, alighted from the cars at no great distance from Ernest's cottage. The great hotel, which had formerly been the palace of Mr. Gathergold, was close at hand, but the poet, with his carpet-bag on his arm, inquired at once where Ernest dwelt, and was resolved to be accepted as his guest.

Approaching the door, he there found the good old man, holding a volume in his hand, which alternately he read, and then, with a finger between leaves, looked lovingly at the Great Stone Face.

"Good evening," said the poet. "Can you give a traveller a night's lodging?"

"Willingly," answered Ernest; and then he added, smiling, "Methinks I never saw the Great Stone Face look so hospitably at a stranger."

The poet sat down on the bench beside him, and he and Ernest talked together. Often had the poet held intercourse with the wittiest and the wisest, but never before with a man like Ernest, whose thoughts and feelings gushed up with such a natural freedom, and who made great truths so familiar by his simple utterance of them. Angels, as had been so often said, seemed to have wrought with him at his labor in the fields; angels seemed to have sat with him by the fireside; and, dwelling with angels as friend with friends, he had imbibed the sublimity of their ideas, and imbued it with the sweet and lowly charm of household words. So thought the poet. And Ernest, on the other hand, was moved and agitated by the living images which the poet flung out of his mind, and which peopled all the air about the cottage door with shapes of beauty, both gay and pensive. The sympathies of these two men instructed them with a profounder sense than either could have attained alone. Their minds accorded into one strain, and made delightful music which neither of them could have claimed as all his own, nor distinguished his own share from the other's. They led one another, as it were, into a high pavilion of their thoughts, so remote, and hitherto so dim, that they had never entered it before, and so beautiful that they desired to be there always.

As Ernest listened to the poet, he imagined that the Great Stone Face was bending forward to listen too. He gazed earnestly into the poet's glowing eyes.

"Who are you, my strangely gifted guest?" he said.

The poet laid his finger on the volume that Ernest had been reading.

"You have read these poems," said he. "You know me, then,—for I wrote them."

Again, and still more earnestly than before, Ernest examined the poet's features; then turned towards the Great Stone Face; then

back, with an uncertain aspect, to his guest. But his countenance fell; he shook his head and sighed.

"Wherefore are you sad?" inquired the poet.

"Because," replied Ernest, "all though life I have awaited the fulfillment of a prophecy; and, when I read these poems, I hoped that it might be fulfilled in you."

"You hoped," answered the poet, faintly smiling, "to find in me the likeness of the Great Stone Face. And you are disappointed, as formerly with Mr. Gathergold, and Old Blood-and-Thunder, and Old Stony Phiz. Yes, Ernest, it is my doom. You must add my name to the illustrious three, and record another failure of your hopes. For—in shame and sadness do I speak it, Ernest—I am not worthy to be typified by yonder benign and majestic image."

"And why?" asked Ernest. He pointed to the volume. "Are not those thoughts divine?"

"They have a strain of the Divinity," replied the poet. "You can hear in them the far-off echo of a heavenly song. But my life, dear Ernest, has not corresponded with my thought. I have had grand dreams, but they have been only dreams, because I have lived—and that, too by my own choice—

among poor and mean realities. Sometimes even—shall I dare to say it?—I lack faith in the grandeur, the beauty, and the goodness which my own works are said to have made more evident in nature and in human life. Why, then, pure seeker of the good and true, shouldst thou hope to find me in yonder image of the divine?"

The poet spoke sadly, and his eyes were dim with tears. So likewise, were those of Ernest.

At the hour of sunset, as had long been his frequent custom, Ernest was to discourse to an assemblage of the neighboring inhabitants, in the open air. He and the poet, arm in arm, still talking together as they went along, proceeded to the spot. It was a small nook among the hills, with a gray precipice behind, the stern front of which was relieved by the pleasant foliage of many creeping plants, that made a tapestry for the naked rock, by hanging their festoons from all its rugged angles. At a small elevation above the ground, set in a rich framework of verdure, there appeared a niche, spacious enough to admit a human figure, with freedom for such gestures as spontaneously accompany earnest thought and genuine emotion. Into this natural pulpit Ernest ascended, and threw a look of familiar kindness around upon his audience. They stood, or sat, or reclined upon the grass, as seemed good to each, with the departing sunshine falling obliquely over them, and mingling its subdued cheerfulness with the solemnity of a grove of ancient trees, beneath and amid the boughs of which the golden rays were constrained to pass. In another direction was seen the Great Stone Face, with the same cheer, combined with the same solemnity, in its benignant aspect.

Ernest began to speak, giving to the people of what was in his heart and mind. His words had power, because they accorded with his thoughts; and his thoughts had reality and depth, because they harmonized with the life which he had always lived. It was not mere breath that this preacher uttered; they were the words of life, because a life of good deeds and holy love was melted into them. Pearls; pure and rich, had been dissolved into this precious draught. The poet, as he listened, felt that the being and character of Ernest were a nobler strain of poetry than he had ever written. His eyes glistening with tears, he gazed reverentially at the venerable man, and said within himself that never was there an aspect so worthy of a prophet and a sage as that mild, sweet, thoughtful countenance, with the glory of white hair diffused about it. At a distance, but distinctly to be seen, high up in the golden light of the setting sun, appeared the Great Stone Face, with hoary mists around it, like the white hairs around the brow of Ernest. Its look of grand beneficence seemed to embrace the world.

At that moment, in sympathy with a thought which he was about to utter, the face of Ernest assumed a grandeur of expression, so imbued with benevolence, that the poet, by an irresistible impulse, threw his arms aloft, and shouted,—

"Behold! Behold! Ernest is himself the likeness of the Great Stone Face!"

Then all the people looked, and saw that what the deep-sighted poet said was true. The prophecy was fulfilled. But Ernest, having finished what he had to say, took the poet's arm, and walked slowly homeward, still hoping that some wiser and better man than himself would by and by appear, bearing a resemblance to the Great Stone Face.

_____ read

"The Great Stone Face,"

by Nathaniel Hawthorne

with _____

on: _____ (date)

The special poet who came to visit the old Ernest seemed to be a very nice person.
How can we find out his name?
It would be fun to search for it.

Old Man Math

THE OLD MAN was created by nature thousands of years ago. In 1850 Nathaniel Hall was with a group of men who were building a road. He went out to hunt partridges for breakfast. He didn't see any partridges but he did see a profile of a man way up on Cannon Mountain. He ran back to the men he was working with and told them what he saw. From that time on many, many people came to see New Hampshire's Old Man of the Mountain. The Old Man was special. He lived a long, long time. He was happy Nathaniel Hawthorne wrote a story about him. Nathaniel Hawthorne had children and he knew reading was an important way to teach children. He also knew arithmetic was important too. After we know how to add, subtract, multiply and divide we can solve puzzles using numbers. We call this subject in school, mathematics. You're not supposed to know the answer right away so try not to let that part of mathematics upset you. You are supposed to figure out the puzzle. It's fun to work with a friend. Here are some statistics to help you get started.

The Old Man of the Mountain Statistics

The BROW: was about 11 feet
The NOSE: was about 10 Feet
The UPPER LIP: was about 7 feet
The CHIN: was about 12 feet
BROW to CHIN: was a little over 40 feet

On the next page is a word puzzle. Try to figure the answer. You can try it alone or with a friend.

Puzzle Page

There are 5,280 feet in a mile so the Old Man was not a mile high on Cannon Mountain. In the year 2000 when our Old Man was still on Cannon Mountain a climber climbed only ten feet a minute because of the steepness. **ABOUT** how long did it take that climber to reach the Old Man's chin?

Hint: Assume the top of the Old Man's head was 1,200 feet high. The Old Man statistics are on page 43.

* Just for fun, write some more word puzzles for someone to solve.